NADO, 2011

I SURVIVED

THE DESTRUCTION OF POMPEII, AD 79

THE BATTLE OF GETTYSBURG, 1863

THE GREAT CHICAGO FIRE, 1871

THE SAN FRANCISCO EARTHQUAKE, 1906

THE SINKING OF THE *TITANIC*, 1912

THE SHARK ATTACKS OF 1916

THE BOMBING OF PEARL HARBOR, 1941

THE NAZI INVASION, 1944

THE ATTACKS OF SEPTEMBER 11, 2001

HURRICANE KATRINA, 2005

THE JAPANESE TSUNAMI, 2011

I SURVIVED

THE JOPLIN TORNADO, 2011

by Lauren Tarshis

illustrated by Scott Dawson

Scholastic Inc.

Text copyright © 2015 by Lauren Tarshis
Illustrations copyright © 2015 by Scholastic Inc.
All rights reserved. Published by Scholastic Inc., *Publishers since 1920*.
SCHOLASTIC and associated logos are trademarks and/or
registered trademarks of Scholastic Inc.

ISBN 978-0-545-65848-5

20 19 18   19

Printed in the U.S.A.   40
First printing 2015
Designed by Yaffa Jaskoll
Series design by Tim Hall

To the people of Joplin, Missouri

CHAPTER 1

SUNDAY, MAY 22, 2011
5:42 P.M.
JOPLIN, MISSOURI

A monster EF-5 tornado was destroying the city of Joplin, Missouri. And eleven-year-old Dexter James was in its killer grip.

The tornado had snuck up on the city, hiding behind a wall of storm clouds. Few knew it was coming. And nobody imagined that within minutes, it would kill 158 people and destroy much of the city.

In the hours before, Joplin had hummed with happy life. Cheers rose up from Little League fields. Gardens bloomed with roses and wild strawberries. Churches echoed with prayers and hymns.

It was a typical Sunday afternoon.

Until the day turned dark and the wind began to howl.

And then the sky exploded like a bomb.

The tornado was three-quarters of a mile wide, with winds that topped 200 miles per hour. It swept away houses and blasted the wreckage thousands of feet into the sky. It tore apart schools and sent stores crashing down on the people inside. Cars flew through the air. Trucks turned into missiles. Century-old trees were ripped from the ground.

The tornado sirens wailed.

People rushed to their basements and huddled in bathtubs as their houses collapsed on top of them. Parents gripped their children as cruel winds tried to tear them away. In minutes, entire neighborhoods lay in ruins.

Dex was in an SUV when the tornado hit, and now he was trapped.

The ferocious winds roared and sent tree limbs and rocks smashing against the SUV.

And then,

Smash!

A window shattered. The tornado's fury blasted into the SUV. Dex was attacked by swirling winds filled with bits of wood and metal and glass. The pain was like being stung by thousands of scorpions, over and over again.

And then the wind grabbed hold of Dex. It wrapped around him like invisible tentacles, pulling him toward the open window.

Dex had always wanted to see a tornado for real.

And now here it was — the evil, swirling darkness.

Dex was being sucked into the tornado, and he knew there could be no escape.

CHAPTER 2

Dex pedaled his bike through the quiet streets of his neighborhood, his dog, Zeke, trotting right beside him. He was studying an arrow-shaped cloud in the bright blue sky when squealing shouts echoed from just ahead.

"Dexter! Dexter! Buy some lemonade!"

Two identical blond heads bounced up over a rosebush.

It was the little Tucker twins, Stephanie and Bobbie.

Dex wasn't thirsty, but no way could he just ignore the girls. Dex's parents and Mr. Tucker had all grown up together in Joplin. Before the twins were born, Mrs. Tucker worked at Joplin High School, where Mom and Dad both taught math.

There were about 50,000 people living in Joplin, and it seemed that at least half of them were practically part of Dex's family.

Dex stopped his bike in the Tuckers' driveway and dug a quarter out of his pocket. Both girls pointed at Zeke and giggled. The dog sat patiently with his tongue hanging almost down to the ground. Dex had to laugh, too. Poor Zekie was probably the ugliest dog in southwestern Missouri. Dad had it right when he said Zeke looked like a cross between a dolphin and a hyena. But who needed good looks when you were the best dog on the planet?

Dex choked down a Dixie Cup filled with warm, watery lemonade.

"Delicious," he said, smacking his lips.

The little girls beamed, flashing their missing front teeth.

Just then, Mr. Tucker came through the front door. He was lugging two suitcases, which he dropped next to the car.

"Good morning, Dex!" he said, striding over.

"Hey, Mr. Tucker. Going somewhere exciting?"

Mr. Tucker smiled. "Just down to Arkansas, visiting the cousins. We'll be back Monday."

He gave Zeke a pat on the head. "You and your guard dog can keep the burglars away for us."

Dex laughed. The only criminals in this neighborhood were the raccoons that knocked over their garbage cans.

"So," Mr. Tucker said, lowering his voice. "Any word from Jeremy?"

The question punched Dex in the gut.

Jeremy, Dex's twenty-year-old brother, was a member of the US Navy SEALs, a special part of the military. He was overseas on a mission, but Dex had no idea where. SEAL missions were top secret. Jeremy could be anywhere in the world where there was a war to fight, terrorists to catch, or hostages to rescue.

"No news yet," Dex said, his throat tightening up. Jeremy had warned him that he could be out of touch for weeks during his mission. But still, each day without hearing Jeremy's voice felt like a year.

When Jeremy first became a SEAL, all Dex felt was pride. His brother was one of the toughest warriors on the whole planet! How awesome was that? Folks in Joplin said Jeremy was a hero. At school, even Dylan Elliott and his pals were coming up to Dex, dying to know every detail about being a SEAL.

Dylan and Dex used to be close buddies. But over the years, Dylan had spent more and more time with guys from his baseball team. Dylan and Dex never had a fight, or even exchanged a mean look. But somehow an invisible wall had risen up between them, and Dex had no idea how to break it down.

And so it was a happy surprise for Dex that suddenly Dylan and his pals wanted to sit with

7

him at lunch. They'd crowd around him, begging to see the picture of Jeremy in his night-vision goggles with his M16 rifle strapped to his chest. They'd ignore their chocolate milk and French toast sticks as Dex told them everything Jeremy could do: parachute into a war zone, scuba dive one hundred feet down into the sea, survive an arctic blizzard or desert sandstorm.

"Did he ever have to eat a raw lizard?" asked Mike Sturm, who had replaced Dex as Dylan's best friend.

"Quiet, Mike," Dylan snapped. "They don't eat lizards, do they, Dex?"

"No," Dex said. "They can eat some kinds of bugs, though. They're really high in protein."

That sent them all into fits of groaning giggles, and the happy sounds echoed through Dex's mind all day. He hadn't realized how much he'd missed Dylan, and how good it would feel to be one of the guys.

But over the past couple of weeks, something strange had happened to Dex. He didn't want to tell stories about Jeremy. He didn't want to *think* about Jeremy. Because it had suddenly dawned on Dex that his brother — his best friend in the world — might not make it home in one piece. Jeremy could get shot, blown up, kidnapped . . . or worse. Last night, Dex had lain sweating in his bed, actually counting the ways his brother could get hurt.

Dex couldn't admit this to the guys; they'd think he was a little coward.

And he sure didn't want to talk about it with Mr. Tucker right now. He said a quick good-bye, afraid he was going to start blubbering in front of the twins.

As Dex rode toward home with Zeke, his brain flashed with nightmare thoughts.

There was Jeremy, pinned against a mountainside as grenades exploded all around him.

There was Jeremy, leaping out of a burning Black Hawk helicopter.

There was Jeremy, alone and bleeding in some far-off desert.

Dex pedaled faster, as though his terror was a ferocious beast he could speed away from.

He flew down the street on his bike.
He ignored the stop sign.
He barely heard the horn or the screeching tires.
And then,
Bam!
Dex was flying through the air.

CHAPTER 3

Crash!

Dex hit the pavement. It took him a few long seconds to realize what had happened.

It wasn't the car that had knocked him down.

It was Zeke!

The dog had smacked into the bike, sending Dex tumbling to the street seconds before the car would have hit him.

Dex sat there in shock until Zeke revived him with an attack of slobbering licks.

"You saved me," Dex said, burying his face in Zeke's smooth gray fur.

Dex was still catching his breath when a man came rushing toward him. Dex realized that it was the owner of the car that had almost hit him.

Dex hauled himself to his feet.

"Are you okay?!" the man asked breathlessly. "I think that dog of yours might have super-powers! Did he actually push you off that bike?"

"I think he did," Dex said, staring at the man. There was something familiar about his shiny bald head and friendly brown eyes.

Wait . . . no . . . could it be?

Dex's heart started to pound.

"You're Doctor Norman Gage," Dex blurted out. "The storm chaser!"

"That's right," the man said with a surprised laugh.

Dr. Gage had his own TV show, called *Tornado Mysteries*. Dad and Dex watched it every week. Jeremy had loved it, too. What was extra cool was that Dad had actually known Dr. Gage in college. Dad always regretted that they'd lost touch.

"I'm Dex James," Dex said, trying not to squeak with excitement like one of the Tucker twins. "I think you maybe know my father, David."

Dr. Gage studied Dex with a confused look, but then he burst into a big grin.

"You're kidding me! You're Dave James's son!" he said. "I miss that guy! Your dad is one of the smartest people I've ever met!"

"I love your show," Dex gushed.

"Ha!" Dr. Gage said. "And to think I almost ran over my only fan."

"No! My dad and brother love your show, too."

"That makes my day," Dr. Gage said, and Dex could see he really meant it.

Dex looked over at Dr. Gage's vehicle, which he recognized now from the show. It was a bright red SUV with thick tires and a forest of antennas sprouting from the roof. It looked more like a tank than a regular car.

"What are you doing here in Joplin?" Dex asked.

Dex knew that Dr. Gage lived in Tulsa, Oklahoma, which was a good two hours away.

"There's a workshop I'm going to this evening," Dr. Gage said. "But I'm going to stay over and do

some storm chasing tomorrow. There's an interesting storm brewing to the west of here."

"You think we'll get a tornado?" Dex asked.

They got plenty of storms every spring, violent thunderstorms that turned the sky black and sent down sheets of rain. There were tornado warnings practically every week. But there hadn't been a big tornado in Joplin in forty years.

"You never know for sure when a tornado is going to strike," Dr. Gage said. "But I've been tracking this storm all week. From the way things are looking, I think we could get a tornado somewhere north of Galena."

Galena was about seven miles from Joplin, just over the Kansas border.

Dex felt a mix of fear and excitement.

"I've always wanted to see a tornado," he blurted out.

Not a big one, of course, and not up close. He understood that tornadoes are one of the most destructive forces in nature. Powerful tornadoes are like mile-wide chain saws, with winds that can get up to 300 miles per hour, strong enough to pulverize buildings, turn a neighborhood into a pile of wood chips, or pick up a tractor trailer and hurl it a hundred yards.

Tornadoes were terrifying. But they were fascinating, too, like Komodo dragons and black mamba snakes.

And Dex had always wanted to see one with his own eyes, not just in YouTube videos and on Dr. Gage's show.

"Tell you what," Dr. Gage said. "Why don't you and your dad come along with me tomorrow?

I can't guarantee we'll see anything — most times I don't. But there's always something new to learn."

Dex's heart leaped up, but then he remembered that both Mom and Dad had to go to the Joplin High School graduation tomorrow. All of the teachers had to be there.

"My dad won't be able to come," Dex said.

Dr. Gage reached into his pocket and took out a business card, which he handed to Dex.

"Have my old buddy give me a call. Maybe he'll let you come and help me out."

Dr. Gage gave Zeke a last pat on the head and got into his SUV.

Dex blinked his eyes hard, sure this was all a dream.

But no! He had been invited to go storm chasing with Dr. Norman Gage.

He might actually see a tornado, for real.

CHAPTER 4

THAT NIGHT
7:00 P.M.

"Sounds way too dangerous," Mom said, adding a dash of pepper to a bubbling pot of chili. "I don't like the idea of Dex heading off with some thrill seeker."

Dex, Mom, and Dad were in the kitchen, cooking their usual Saturday night chili dinner. Dad had already spoken to Dr. Gage and he was excited for Dex to go on tomorrow's chase. Now they just had to get Mom to go along with the plan.

"Deb, Norm is a serious scientist," Dad said.

Mom eyed him. "What he does is dangerous, David. Norman Gage isn't chasing bunnies. He's chasing tornadoes!"

"Now there's a show I'd like to see," Dad said. "Norman Gage, bunny chaser!"

That made them all laugh, with Mom's singsong giggle rising up loudest.

Good sign, Dex thought. When Mom was really upset, not even Zeke could make her smile. After Jeremy left, it seemed Mom hadn't cracked a smile for a month.

Mom stopped laughing. "I'd just feel better if one of us were going along."

There was no way she or Dad could miss the graduation ceremony.

Dad brushed one of Mom's blond curls off of her forehead. "I trust Norm. He really doesn't take risks," Dad said. "And this is an incredible opportunity for Dex."

"You should see his car, Mom," Dex said. "It can go way faster than any tornado."

Mom looked at Dad, and then Dex, flicking her dark eyes back and forth. Dex held his breath.

Finally, Mom gave her *I surrender* sigh and flashed the smile that Dad swore was the prettiest in Joplin.

"All right."

Victory!

After dinner, Mom put the Scrabble board on the table. She looked at Dex hopefully.

"Quick game?"

Scrabble used to be another Saturday night tradition — Mom and Dad versus Dex and Jeremy. The fierce games would stretch for hours over bowls of popcorn and chocolate ice cream. When Dex and Jeremy won, they'd parade around the house like Super Bowl champs, whooping with joy.

Dex couldn't tell Mom that with Jeremy gone, Scrabble was just a boring game. He kissed her good night. "I need to get a good night's sleep for tomorrow."

He said good night to Dad and headed up to his room.

He watched a couple episodes of Dr. Gage's show and then got ready for bed. He pulled back his blankets to make a spot for Zeke. He had to yank hard to undo his sheets, which were tucked in extra tight.

Jeremy had taught him how to make his bed that way. He had just finished SEAL training in California, the most brutal military training in the world. It was six months of pure misery, Jeremy said, endless days of grueling runs, freezing ocean swims, and impossible obstacle courses.

The worst night for Jeremy was when they had to swim for hours in the freezing Pacific Ocean. The surf was so rough he got thrown against some rocks and cut his leg.

"They finally pulled me out of the water," Jeremy had said. "They were afraid my blood would attract the great white sharks that feed in that area."

Dex had repeated that story to Dylan and the guys, and they had almost fallen off of their chairs with happiness.

Dex also showed them Jeremy's SEAL trident pin, which Jeremy let him bring to school for the day. The pin was a golden eagle clutching an anchor, a gun, and a three-pronged spear. Dex explained that out of the 118 guys who started in Jeremy's training class, only 23 passed and got their pins.

The guys crowded around Dex, staring at the pin in awe, as if it was a dinosaur egg about to hatch.

"What was the best thing Jeremy learned in training?" Dylan had asked.

Almost without thinking, Dex said, "To make his bed right. It's the first thing a SEAL learns in training. Anyone who does it wrong gets their bed ripped apart by the instructors."

"I don't get it," Dylan said, not rudely.

Dex had said the same thing to Jeremy, and now Dex repeated his brother's answer almost word for word to the guys.

"Because you make your bed right, and you've started your day doing something right. And if you have a hard day, you can come home to a bed you made, so you can go to sleep and get strong again for the next day."

The guys watched for Dylan's reaction.

"That makes sense," he said finally.

And now Dex climbed into his perfectly made bed and snuggled up with Zeke. He said a silent good night to his brother, and a prayer to keep him safe.

Tonight, at least, he didn't lie awake thinking about Jeremy.

His head was filled with tornadoes dancing in the sky, touching down in his mind and carrying him off to sleep.

CHAPTER 5

THE NEXT DAY
MAY 22
1:30 P.M.

Mom was tutoring one of her students after church, so it was just Dad and Dex waiting on the porch when Dr. Gage zoomed into the driveway. He hopped out of the SUV and came rushing over to Dad. They hugged each other like long-lost brothers. Zeke seemed happy to see Dr. Gage, too.

Of course Dad insisted on a personal tour of Dr. Gage's SUV, which had been specially equipped for storm chasing. There were the extra-strong metal plates bolted to the sides to protect from flying rocks and debris. There were oversized tires for driving at high speeds across flooded fields and rocky ditches. The cluster of antennas gave Dr. Gage instant access to the latest weather data.

And that was just the outside. Inside were three different computer screens, all mounted to the dashboard. There was even a mini freezer in the back.

"For keeping hailstones frozen," Dr. Gage explained, grinning like a kid showing off a new LEGO set.

When they finished with the tour, Dr. Gage told them about their plan for the day. He and Dex would be chasing a big storm that was charging in from the west.

"It's already a supercell."

Dex knew that supercells were the most violent and dangerous thunderstorms, the storms that could unleash tornadoes.

"We'll head over to Galena and see if we can catch it as it heads north."

And Dr. Gage had a surprise for them. "Dex will be helping me with a research project."

It turned out Dr. Gage had been working with a team of scientists.

"We're trying to figure out if a tornado makes a sound just as it's beginning to form inside a storm."

"The cry of a baby tornado," Dad said.

Dr. Gage chuckled. "In a way. We believe some animals can sense when a tornado is coming, long before it touches down. Our theory is that they can detect sounds that we humans can't hear."

"Fascinating," Dad said.

"If there really are these sounds, and we can find a way to detect them, we could have much earlier warning before tornadoes touch down."

"Tell us about the research," Dad said.

Dr. Gage's face lit up. He hit a button on his key chain, which popped open the tailgate of his SUV. Inside was a large cardboard box filled with metal balls. Each was the size of an apple.

"I call these sound pods," said Dr. Gage, handing one to Dad and one to Dex. "Each has a little recording instrument inside."

The metal ball was surprisingly light.

"How do you get them up into the storm clouds?" Dad asked.

"That's the fun part," Dr. Gage said. He reached behind the box and brought out what looked like a toy rifle.

"It used to be a paintball gun," Dr. Gage said. "I tinkered with it, added a wider barrel. So now it's my official sound-pod launcher."

He loaded one of the silver balls into the barrel and handed the rifle to Dad.

"Give it a try," he said.

Dad smiled excitedly as he aimed the rifle into the blue sky.

He pulled the trigger.

Phfffft!

The ball hissed out of the gun, a silver blur. And then,

Pop!

A small balloon inflated in the sky, like a mini parachute. But instead of drifting down, the balloon shot up farther into the sky.

"The balloon will lift the sound recorder up

about ten thousand feet," Dr. Gage explained. "And the sounds are transmitted back to my lab. So far I've collected sounds from fifteen different storms."

"Any theories yet?" Dad asked.

"Some," Dr. Gage said, looking at Dad. "Sure you can't come along today?"

Dad shook his head sadly. "The graduation starts at three," he said. "But how about you join us for dinner tonight? We can talk more then."

Dr. Gage agreed, and they said their good-byes. Dex couldn't decide who looked sadder about being left behind, Dad or the dog.

Dr. Gage turned on the engine, and the three computer screens came to life. Dex studied the screen in front of him, which showed a weather radar map. Splotches of different colors pulsed on the screen like jellyfish.

"There's our storm," Dr. Gage said, pointing to a patch of bloodred.

His eyes narrowed.

"It's going to be a monster."

CHAPTER 6

They headed out through the downtown, the oldest part of Joplin.

"I love this street," Dr. Gage said, admiring the brick and stone buildings that had been watching over Main Street for more than a hundred years.

"That used to be my great-grandfather's diner," Dex said as they passed a squat brick building that was now a gift shop.

"How long has your family been in Joplin?" Dr. Gage asked.

"Since 1925," Dex said. "My great-grandfather came here when he was sixteen."

Dr. Gage raised his eyebrows.

"You're Joplin royalty," Dr. Gage said.

Dex had to laugh as he imagined a king eating Mom's Saturday night chili, or a princess lounging on the couch covered with Zeke's fur. Dex loved his house. But it wasn't exactly a castle.

"I bet Joplin is a great place to grow up," Dr. Gage said.

"It is." Dex nodded, surprised how much he meant it.

Sure, there were more exciting places. Mike Sturm was always bragging about his family trips to New York City, where the buildings scraped against the clouds, or Las Vegas, where wild parties lasted all night. In Joplin, the tallest rooftops were mostly the church steeples, and the best parties were backyard barbecues.

Dex knew that one day he'd travel the world. But he also knew he'd always be happy to come home to Joplin.

The land flattened out as they drove toward Kansas, and soon there was nothing but bright green cornfields. Dex scanned the sky, which was clear blue except for some hazy clouds. It was hard to imagine that a violent storm was somewhere nearby.

They came upon a beat-up pickup truck on the side of the road, at the edge of a field. A young man and woman were standing there, video cameras aimed up at a patch of gray clouds. Dex guessed they were storm chasers, too.

Dr. Gage smiled wide as he pulled up next to them and rolled down his window.

"Jimmy! Sara! How are you?" he called out.

"Norm!" the two chorused.

"Hey, Jimmy, how's the leg?" Dr. Gage asked.

"Thirty stitches, Norm. But healing up nice."

"Sara, keep your buddy out of trouble today, will you? I want you guys to be careful."

"We promise, Norm," said Sara, her brown eyes shining out through round glasses. "Who's your assistant?"

"This is Dex James. His dad and I went to college together."

Dex was relieved Dr. Gage didn't reveal how

they'd met yesterday — with Dex almost getting squashed by Dr. Gage's SUV.

"Dex," Jimmy said. "You know you're chasing with one of the best guys in the world."

Dex smiled.

"We're heading northwest," Dr. Gage said. "What about you?"

"We'll probably see you later," Sara said. "You going to get some pods into the sky?"

"We're about to," Dr. Gage said. "You both take care. And, seriously, be careful!"

After they'd driven away, Dr. Gage told Dex how Jimmy got his thirty stitches.

"Last month, he and Sara were chasing in Mississippi, and they got too close to an EF-5 tornado."

Dex knew that EF-5 tornadoes are the strongest tornadoes, according to a system called the Enhanced Fujita Scale, which scientists use to rate the strength of tornadoes. An EF-1 is the weakest — a breeze funnel or little rope tornado that can knock over a chicken coop but not much else. The EF-5s are the killers, the violent twisters that wipe out whole towns.

"The wind shifted," Dr. Gage explained, "and the tornado they were chasing started chasing them. Their car got thrown, and Jimmy sliced open his leg. Luckily the tornado changed direction again and missed them. But they could have been killed."

Dr. Gage shook his head like a worried father.

"I'm hoping they learned their lesson," he added.

"Do you really think we're going to see tornadoes today?" Dex asked, suddenly wondering if that's what he really wanted.

"We can never be sure, not even with our radar and satellites and computers. All we can do is warn that a tornado *might* strike, and usually we're wrong."

That sure was true in Joplin. The tornado sirens went off practically every week, always false alarms. They were like watchdogs that growled at every squirrel. Most people in Joplin ignored the sirens.

"Can't you a see a tornado on the radar?" Dex asked.

"No," Dr. Gage said. "You can see clues — high wind speeds, a storm that has what we call *rotation*, or spinning clouds. But tornadoes form deep inside the clouds, hidden from satellites and radar. We don't know a tornado is coming until someone actually sees it with their own eyes."

Dex glanced out the window, half expecting a black funnel to explode out of the sky.

Dr. Gage went on. "But the most dangerous tornadoes are the ones you can't see. They hide behind walls of rain and clouds and nobody can see them coming."

"Those are called rain-wrapped tornadoes, right?" Dex asked.

Dex was showing off; he'd learned that term on Dr. Gage's show.

"Yes. We call them black walls of death."

Dex didn't like the sound of that.

"Have you ever been up close to one of those?"

Dr. Gage didn't answer at first.

"Too close," he said finally, looking at Dex.

He pulled up the sleeve of his shirt, and Dex tried not to gasp. There was a thick purple scar zigzagging from Dr. Gage's wrist up to his elbow, as though a monster had tried to chew off his arm.

"What happened?" Dex asked.

Dr. Gage took a deep breath. And then, as they drove through the cornfields of Kansas, Dr. Gage told Dex the story of the tornado that nearly killed him.

CHAPTER 7

"It was Wednesday, April third, 1974," Dr. Gage began. "My eleventh birthday. I got a brand-new bike, and after school all I wanted to do was ride around town to show it off."

Dr. Gage grew up in a small Alabama town called Jasper, with his parents and two little sisters.

"Beautiful place. Quiet and friendly. A little like Joplin."

The day was hot and very humid, not unusual for Alabama in the springtime. There were thunderstorms forecast all around the South, up into Ohio. That wasn't so unusual, either.

But there was nothing usual about these storms. They were supercells. While Dr. Gage was happily riding his bike along the peaceful streets of Jasper, storms were already unleashing tornadoes for hundreds of miles in every direction.

Boom!

A tornado touched down in Cleveland, Tennessee, destroying the entire downtown.

Boom!

Another took aim at Xenia, Ohio, wiping out a neighborhood of brick houses, destroying a high school, and killing thirty-two people.

Boom, boom, boom!

Tornadoes struck in Kentucky, Indiana, and Georgia.

At five fifteen, the skies in Jasper grew suddenly dark, and it began to pour.

"I figured it was just a thunderstorm. I was more worried about my bike getting rusty than anything else."

The town had no tornado siren, so Dr. Gage had no way of knowing that a massive, rain-wrapped tornado was heading right for him.

"I pulled to the side of the road to wait out the storm. I waited there under a tree, thinking about the cake my mother was making for me. It started to hail, huge stones that pounded down. My ears started to pop like crazy. I didn't know that was a sign that a tornado was coming. The air pressure is so low inside a tornado that the sudden change in pressure makes your ears pop, like when you're in an airplane."

Dex had never heard that.

"And then there was a sound, like nothing I'd ever heard before. Most people say that a tornado sounds like a speeding freight train. But every tornado sounds different. This one was roaring and hissing, like some kind of snake. Stuff started flying through the air — leaves, branches, and roof shingles. That's when I realized what was happening."

"What did you do?" Dex asked.

"There was a big ditch right at the side of the road. I dove in and wedged myself under the root of a huge tree, held on for dear life. I got pummeled pretty badly. A tractor came flying out of the sky, and crashed down about ten feet from me. The tree I had been standing under was ripped out of the ground. My arm got sliced by a hunk of steel pipe that hit me at one hundred fifty miles per hour."

Dex shuddered.

"But I was incredibly lucky," Dr. Gage said. "I made it. And so did my parents and my sisters. They rode out the storm in our basement. The house was pretty much destroyed. But we felt blessed. Twenty-three people in our town were killed, including two of my friends."

It turned out that the EF-3 tornado that hit Jasper was part of what would become known as the Super Outbreak of 1974. Over twenty-four hours, 148 tornadoes touched down in thirteen states. By the time the skies had cleared, more than 330 people were dead.

"You'd think that after that, I'd stay as far away from tornadoes as I could. But I decided to learn everything about them. I became obsessed. The more we know about tornadoes, the better we will be able to predict when and where they'll hit. You know, last month, there was another super outbreak of tornadoes, all across the South. That's where Jimmy and Sara got caught. It was as bad as the one in 1974 — we lost three hundred twenty-one people. So we haven't made much progress, Dex. We need a much better early warning system so that people aren't caught by surprise."

Something in Dr. Gage's voice — a steely edge — reminded Dex of Jeremy, how he sounded when he talked about his missions. They were alike, Dex realized. Both were trying to make the world safer. But both were risking their lives.

Both were hunting killers.

Dex wanted to know more about what had happened to Dr. Gage that day.

But just then Dr. Gage pointed out the window at a whirl of thick gray clouds rushing in from the west.

"There it is!" he exclaimed.

It was their storm.

The chase was on.

CHAPTER 8

They followed the storm east for about three miles, and then they pulled off the road. They got out and stood at the edge of a cornfield.

The air was steamy and thick, and the wind was stronger. The corn plants rippled like waves on a stormy ocean.

They stood for a few minutes, watching as the metal-gray cloud grew thicker and darker. Before Dex's eyes, the cloud formed itself into a giant circle. The bottom was perfectly flat, and the top towered up into the sky, as though it would bump into the moon.

Dex thought it looked like a UFO. But Dr. Gage had a more scientific name for it.

"That is a perfect cumulonimbus cloud." He stared in awe. "Those are the clouds that make tornadoes."

Dr. Gage walked to the back of the SUV and popped open the tailgate.

"Let's get some sound pods into the sky," he said, grabbing the rifle. "Would you like to do the shooting?"

Dex took the rifle, trying to act as if it was no big deal.

But inside his brain an excited little voice was screaming, *I get to shoot the pods! I get to shoot the pods!*

Dr. Gage grabbed four of the silver balls.

He took a quick look at the weather radar. "I think the storm is actually losing strength."

Sure enough, that UFO cloud was already melting apart, like gray ice cream left out in the sun.

"But let's shoot some pods up anyway. I'm curious to hear what's going on in there. We'll go into the middle of the field. The winds will be better."

Dr. Gage led Dex into the middle of the cornfield, where stalks rose up past Dex's knees. He helped Dex load the balls into the rifle.

"Pull the trigger four times with about five seconds in between."

Dex aimed up at the cloud.

Phhttt!

Phhttt!

Phhttt!

Phhttt!

Each of the silver balls streaked up into the air, and then,

Pop!

Pop!

Pop!

Pop!

One by one the pods burst open, releasing the balloons. They rose up through the sky, like four brave soldiers ready for a daring mission.

"Perfect!" Dr. Gage exclaimed.

Dex's heart leaped up, and he thought of Jeremy. His brother would love this! Dex could imagine Jeremy's chiming laugh, how his blue eyes would gleam, how they'd talk about this for weeks.

And then came the familiar gut stab of worry, as Dex wondered where on earth his brother was. He closed his eyes, trying to block out the pictures of exploding bombs and burning tanks that flashed through his mind.

And then, *boom!*

For a second, Dex thought a bomb had blasted out of his mind and into the field.

But when he opened his eyes, he saw bolts of lightning tearing open the storm cloud. The cloud had turned black and was billowing like smoke.

Boom!

Dex could actually feel electricity pulsing through the air. The hairs on his arms stood straight up from the shock.

Boom, boom, boom!

Lightning bolts shot out of the cloud, like flaming spears.

Kaboom!

Dr. Gage grabbed Dex's arm. "I was wrong about this storm! It's dangerous. We need to get away from this lightning."

Kaboom!

A tree at the edge of the field got hit and exploded into millions of pieces.

The skies burst open, and rain came pouring down in sheets. In seconds Dex's hair and clothes were soaked. He ran with Dr. Gage, slipping in the mud, blinking away the raindrops that splashed into his eyes.

And then came the hail.

The stones were small at first, but soon Dex and Dr. Gage were being pummeled by big rocks.

"Cover your head!" Dr. Gage boomed.

Dex put his hands over his head, but it didn't help. It was like getting hit by baseballs pitched at a hundred miles an hour.

They were just a few feet from the car when a huge hailstone smashed into Dex. He saw a burst of stars, and next thing he knew, he was on the ground.

CHAPTER 9

Dr. Gage helped Dex up and practically dragged him to the car.

By the time Dex was in his seat, the hail had stopped.

Dr. Gage opened the glove compartment and took out a first aid kit. He fished out an ice pack, gave it a good smack, and laid it gently on the painful lump on Dex's scalp.

"You sure you're all right?" Dr. Gage said, his brow crinkled up with worry.

"I'm fine," Dex said, and luckily he was. He just hoped that Mom wouldn't find out.

"I am so sorry, Dex. I never should have put us in the middle of that field. From the radar, I actually thought the storm was going to lose power. I should have known better."

"I think your car is in worse shape than me," Dex said. A hailstone had turned the windshield into a spiderweb of cracks.

Dr. Gage laughed. "I've had it replaced twice this year already."

They sat for a few minutes until the rain stopped.

"It always surprises me," Dr. Gage said. "Nature can be so violent one minute, and so peaceful the next. And we humans have no control at all."

Dr. Gage opened his door and stepped outside.

A few seconds later he came back holding a huge hailstone, perfectly round and glistening.

He presented it to Dex as though it was a priceless diamond. "A souvenir."

It was very light and smooth. Dex brought it up to his nose and sniffed it. It smelled musty, and he caught a whiff of something strangely familiar.

Dr. Gage seemed to read his mind. "Mint, right?"

"That's it!" Dex said.

"I wish I could tell you why. We can put it in my little freezer until we get home."

Dex had already decided he'd bring it to school tomorrow. He'd pack it in a small cooler and show it to the guys at lunch. Dylan would freak!

Dr. Gage turned his attention to the weather radar map. He pointed at two red blotches pulsing across the screen.

"Look at these," he said with surprise. "There are two new storms heading this way. Both are supercells."

His face darkened.

"It's going to get dangerous around here when all of these storms come together. Jimmy and Sara love this kind of weather. But I think it's too risky to be out chasing. I can't tell where these storms are heading, and how strong they're going to get."

He looked at Dex apologetically.

"I think we should head back to Joplin, call it a day."

"That's fine," Dex said, trying not to sound too relieved.

That lightning had spooked him, and that hailstone had almost cracked open his skull.

He'd seen enough bad weather for one day.

Dex relaxed on the ride back to Joplin as Dr. Gage told him funny stories about himself and Dad in college. But as they got closer to Dex's neighborhood, Dr. Gage got quiet. He kept one eye on the radar map, and kept glancing warily into the rearview mirror. Was someone following them? Was Dr. Gage going to get a speeding ticket?

Dex turned around, expecting to see flashing police lights.

There were no cars behind them.

But there was something strange in the sky, an enormous gray cloud moving very quickly toward them.

A shiver of fear jangled Dex's spine.

"Is that a supercell?"

"Could be," Dr. Gage said. "There's so much happening on the radar right now. It's hard to know. It's pretty far back. Let's see if we can take a better look."

He made a quick U-turn so that now they were driving slowly in the opposite direction, toward the cloud. It was very dark, but with a hazy blur in the center. It stretched out across the horizon as far as Dex could see.

Dr. Gage stared through the cracked windshield, scanning the sky like a SEAL searching for enemy shooters.

And then a flash of lightning flared inside the cloud, lighting it up from the inside like an X-ray.

"Oh, my Lord," Dr. Gage whispered.

In that split second of brightness, they had both seen what was hidden inside the storm cloud.

It was a tornado.

An enormous, churning tornado, the biggest Dex had ever imagined.

It was on a path to destroy Joplin.

CHAPTER 10

Dr. Gage turned the SUV around again, and they raced away from the tornado.

He punched 911 into his phone.

A woman's voice came over the speaker.

"Nine-one-one emergency."

"This is Dr. Norman Gage. I'm a storm chaser. There is a massive tornado on the ground in southwest Joplin. It could be a mile wide. And it is rain-wrapped and almost impossible to see. People need to be warned right away!"

Dex's heart pounded. Had he heard right? Could a tornado really be one mile wide?

If the tornado kept going in the same direction, it would wipe out some of the most crowded parts of the city — Dex's school, the St. John's hospital complex, Dex's church, all the stores and supermarkets and fast-food restaurants that lined South Range Line Road . . .

And Dex's neighborhood.

The wind shook the windows of the SUV. The air was filled with leaves, branches, and black roof shingles.

"This is a huge tornado and very strong," Dr. Gage warned. "Please get the sirens going!"

He hung up with the 911 operator and handed the phone to Dex.

"Call your parents," he said. "Tell them both to take cover and to spread the word."

Dex glanced at the time; it was almost 5:40. Were they home from the graduation yet?

With shaking hands, Dex called home.

All he got was a fast busy signal. Same thing when he tried to call Mom's cell, and then Dad's.

Was cell service cut off?

Just then a piercing shriek rang out through the air — finally, the tornado sirens.

Yeeowwwyeeeowwwyeeeoww!

But was it too late?

And would people pay attention?

Would Mom and Dad know to run to the basement? Would Zeke go with them? His dog hated it down there.

How many people in Joplin knew what was coming?

It was now pouring rain, and the gray cloud was completely invisible.

A massive tornado was about to hit Joplin, and nobody could see it.

Dr. Gage's terrifying words came back to Dex.

Black walls of death.

The wind was getting stronger, gusting in howling breaths.

Trees swayed back and forth.

A huge limb broke off and flew across the street.

Dex noticed a new color on the radar map — pink.

"Dr. Gage," he said softly. "What are those pink dots?"

They were scattered across the red blobs like sprinkles.

Dr. Gage glanced at the screen, his face grim.

"Debris," he answered finally.

Debris. It took Dex a few seconds to get it. Those pink dots were pieces of houses and buildings and cars that had been sucked thousands of feet into the sky.

Dex's eyes flooded with tears.

Joplin! His city was being torn to pieces.

Dr. Gage picked up the handset of his ham radio, which would work even when cell service was out.

"Jimmy, Sara, you there?"

There was a loud crackle, and then Sara's voice.

"Norm, where are you? We're heading into Joplin. I wish you could see this! It's massive! We're following it in."

"Stay back!" he said. "It's right behind us, on Twentieth Street!"

Dex gasped as he watched a telephone pole

55

break in half and slam onto the road in front of them. The wires erupted into a spray of sparks.

Dr. Gage dropped the handset and hit the brakes.

"Norm!" Sara called. "Norm!"

The car skidded on the rain-slick road. It whipped around in a circle, around and around, like a sickening carnival ride.

They were heading right for a huge oak tree, and Dex braced himself for a terrible crash. The car swerved at the last minute, and they missed the tree. Instead, they plowed into a chain-link fence, breaking through the metal mesh and finally lurching to a stop.

They sat there for a moment, too stunned to speak.

They were in front of Peter's Garage, where Dad took his car to be fixed.

A chunk of the roof tore away and smacked into the car.

A stop sign shot past them like an arrow.

The wind was really howling now, branches and roof shingles swirling in the air.

Dr. Gage jammed the SUV into reverse and tried to back up.

56

But the car was tangled inside the broken fence.

The sky darkened; the winds howled with fury.

Rocks and branches pounded their windows.

Jimmy's panicked voice crackled on the radio. "Norm! Norm!"

But Dr. Gage was busy trying to free them from the fence.

The wheels spun. The engine whined.

"Come on, come on . . ." Dr. Gage worked desperately to free the car.

At last the car began to move.

He'd done it!

But no. It wasn't Dr. Gage who was moving the car.

It was the wind.

It rocked the car back and forth, up and down.

Suddenly Dex's ears started to pop.

And there was a noise like nothing Dex had ever heard, like thousands of Black Hawk helicopters had exploded from the sky, their engines roaring, their blades whirring.

The tornado.

It had come for them.

CHAPTER 11

All at once, the world shattered.

The rest of the roof flew off of the garage, blew up into thousands of pieces, and was sucked up into the sky. A storm of wood and metal and leaves churned all around them. A lawn mower dropped out of the sky.

They were in the middle of the tornado now, caught in the evil, swirling darkness. Dex's ears popped over and over from the pressure. His eyes felt as if they would burst from his skull.

He watched in horror as the tornado's chainsaw winds pulverized the garage. The cars parked in front bounced across the lot. A horrible stench filled the air — a mix of rotting earth and gas. It burned Dex's nose and throat and made it hard to take a breath.

But the worst part was the noise. The tornado's whirring roar rose up, mixing with the *thud*, *crash*, *smash* of debris pummeling their car.

They had to get away from here!

Dex remembered all of the tornado drills at school, rules that had been hammered into him since kindergarten.

Stay inside!

Get away from windows!

Rush to a basement and or an inside room!

Cover your head!

Dex knew how dangerous it was to be in a car, even an SUV built for storm chasing. A tornado could yank a freight train off its tracks and suck it into the sky. Even a tank was no match for a strong tornado.

But where else could they go? Even if there was an underground bomb shelter right in the parking lot, they couldn't get to it. Stepping outside now would be crazy. They might as well run through a spray of machine-gun fire and grenades.

And then,

Smash!

The window next to Dex shattered, shooting glass across his face.

Whoosh!

The tornado wind blasted into the car, hot air packed with dirt and rocks and wood and glass. It swirled around Dex, biting into his flesh. Dirt shot into his eyes and up his nose.

The wind kept getting stronger, until it seemed that there was an enormous animal in the car with them, an invisible beast with strangling tentacles. It wrapped itself around Dex and pulled him out of his seat, toward the window. His seat belt strained, pressing against his neck like a noose, cutting into his skin. And then it snapped, and Dex went flying toward the open window.

Dr. Gage gripped Dex's arm so hard that Dex was afraid it would be torn off. He pulled Dex back, refusing to let him fall into the tornado's hungry jaws.

With a mighty jerk, Dr. Gage managed to break the grip of the wind and throw Dex to the floor.

"Stay down!" Dr. Gage shouted.

Dex wedged himself under the dashboard, curling into a tight ball.

Roooarrrr!

The tornado bellowed like a beast whose bloody kill had been snatched away.

And now it wanted revenge.

With a furious gust, the wind grabbed the car and flipped it onto its side.

Dex tumbled from his hiding place and smacked against Dr. Gage.

The car flipped again so now they were upside down, and again and again. Each flip threw Dex across the car, slamming his head against the ceiling, bashing his body against the doors, tossing him so he couldn't tell if he was up or down.

The tornado seemed to be toying with the car, like a killer cat playing a game with a dying mouse.

But now the game was over, and the real terror would begin.

The tornado sucked the car off the ground. The metal screeched and groaned. One of the back doors flew off.

This is it, Dex thought. The car was going to get sucked into the sky. He and Dr. Gage would be crushed, or blown thousands of feet into the clouds.

He called out for Mom, for Dad, for Jeremy, but the tornado swallowed his cries.

Dex squeezed his eyes shut and prayed.

There was an explosion, a blinding light, and then nothing.

CHAPTER 12

Dex felt that he was floating gently, drifting through the air like a feather.

It was very dark and quiet.

The tornado must have carried him high into the clouds.

But then Dex started to spin, *faster, faster, faster*.

And now he felt like he was falling.

He reached out, grasping frantically, as though he could grab hold of a star, or a cloud.

Dex's eyes flew open.

And he realized that the spinning was only in his mind.

He was in Dr. Gage's SUV, crumpled across the backseat. The windows were gone. The airbags had opened. There was a huge hole in the roof.

Carefully he moved his arms and legs. He put his hand on his chest, feeling his pounding heart.

Was he actually alive?

He felt like he'd been in a blender, his body beaten to a pulp.

But somehow no part of him had been crushed or broken or torn open.

The tornado had moved on. Dex could hear it in the distance, its roar faded to a distant moan.

He sat up, wincing in pain as he spat out mouthfuls of dirt and grit.

He wiped away the layer of mud and snot and blood that covered his face. And slowly the world around him came into focus.

It was no world he recognized. It was as if he had crash-landed on a distant planet. Instead of grass, the ground was covered with glass and pulverized wood and metal. Instead of mountains, there were hills of tangled debris. The trees looked like skeletons, stripped of their leaves and branches and even their bark.

He was still in the parking lot of Peter's Garage. The car hadn't flown so far after all.

It made no sense that he hadn't been killed.

But nothing made sense.

The garage building was now a heap of crushed concrete. Smashed cars were scattered all around. One had been wrapped around a tree. Downed electrical wires hissed like fiery snakes. A tricycle hung from the branch of a naked tree.

Slowly the fog lifted from Dex's mind, and he realized what else was wrong: Dr. Gage wasn't in the car.

"Dr. Gage!" Dex cried out.

He looked all around, his blood turning to ice when he spotted him.

Dr. Gage was sprawled on the ground just a few yards away.

He wasn't moving.

Dex's stomach lurched, and a numb feeling spread through him.

He climbed out of the SUV through a shattered

window. Part of the chain-link fence was attached to the bottom of the car. That's what had saved them from being sucked into the sky, Dex realized. The fence had anchored them to the ground.

Dex staggered over to Dr. Gage and fell to his knees. Dr. Gage's brown skin had turned ashy gray. With shaking fingers, Dex felt his cheek, which was cold and clammy.

But his chest was moving.

"Dr. Gage," Dex choked.

To his relief, Dr. Gage's eyes fluttered open.

He stared at Dex with reddened eyes.

"Dex," he rasped. "You made it. You made it."

"We both did."

But then Dr. Gage shut his eyes again.

"Dr. Gage! Dr. Gage."

He didn't answer.

Dex could see he was badly hurt. There was a pool of blood spreading under his right leg.

What should he do? Who could help them?

Dex's mind whirled, as though the tornado winds were spinning his thoughts.

All he knew was that he was alone.

His city was gone.

And Dr. Gage was dying.

If he were a tough SEAL, Dex would carry Dr. Gage on his back and march through the wreckage all the way to St. John's hospital.

But Dex was not a battle-toughened SEAL.

He was an eleven-year-old kid who couldn't even hit a baseball.

He had no team of warriors by his side. He barely even had any friends.

Dex sat down on the cold, wet ground and closed his eyes. He wanted to curl up and disappear. But his mind drifted to the stories Jeremy had told him about SEAL training. He could practically feel his big brother's hand on his shoulder, smell his breath, hear his voice speaking quietly in the darkness.

"They barely let you sleep. You're running for miles every day, swimming in that freezing ocean until your body is numb. It's constant pain. Every minute I wanted to quit."

"Why do they make it so hard?" Dex had asked.

"Because the whole point is to show you that you are stronger than you ever imagined. As a SEAL, there will be times when you are terrified, lost, bleeding. But you can't just quit. The guys on your team are depending on you. Your *country* is counting on you. And so no matter how you feel, you need to find the strength to complete your mission."

Dex still hadn't really understood.

But now, sitting in this wrecked parking lot, it started to dawn on him.

No, Dex wasn't a SEAL. He had no golden trident pin, no M16 rifle, no soldiers lined up all around him.

But Dex had a mission.

To help Dr. Gage.

Some strength seeped into his aching body. He stood up and shook off his tears.

If Dex didn't do something right now, Dr. Gage was going to die.

CHAPTER 13

Dex remembered the first aid kit that Dr. Gage kept in his glove compartment. He peered into the car's shattered insides. The computer screens had been sucked away. The air rifle and sound pods were gone, too.

But the first aid kit was still in the glove compartment.

Dex grabbed it and hurried back to Dr. Gage.

Mom had made him take an advanced first-aid class last summer. He'd hated every minute, but now the training came back to him. He unzipped the case, taking a deep breath to calm his hammering heart.

He followed the steps he'd been taught: put on disposable gloves, use scissors to carefully cut away the muddy fabric that stuck to Dr. Gage's wounded leg. He didn't drop the scissors when he saw the gaping gash above Dr. Gage's knee. He didn't vomit at the sight of the blood, or at the sickening gleam of white bone through the open wound.

He thought of Jeremy, imagining that he was right behind him, calmly walking him through the steps.

He ripped open a package of gauze and pressed down as hard as he could. Blood soaked through, so he took more gauze and pressed harder. He kept pressing to try to stop the bleeding.

The minutes crawled by. Dex gripped Dr. Gage's hand tight.

No, he wouldn't let Dr. Gage go. He would hold on to him for dear life, the way Dr. Gage had held on to Dex when the tornado tried to suck him away.

The bleeding slowed and then stopped. Dr. Gage's skin didn't look as gray. His breathing seemed a little steadier.

Dex was putting on a fresh bandage and wrapping it in adhesive tape when he heard the sound of a truck, and slamming doors, and then voices.

A man and woman came running toward him.

Relief poured over Dex as he realized it was Jimmy and Sara.

"We found you!" Sara shouted.

She and Jimmy started to cry when they saw Dr. Gage lying there, surrounded by bloody gauze.

They kneeled down next to him, and Dr. Gage's eyes fluttered open, but then he drifted away again.

Sara turned to Dex.

"Dex, you took care of him?"

Dex nodded.

He'd done all he could.

"You did real good," Jimmy said.

Dex barely managed a nod as he fought back his tears.

Within minutes, they had found a door in the wreckage to use as a stretcher. Dex helped them carefully move Dr. Gage onto the door, and they carried him to the pickup truck.

"I'll ride in the back with Norm," Sara said. "Dex, you get up front with Jimmy."

Dex shook his head.

"I'm not going with you," he said.

He hated to leave Dr. Gage, but Jimmy and Sara would take good care of him.

"I need to find my mom and dad. I need to get home."

The word *home* caught in his throat.

"I don't live far from here," he said. His neighborhood was no more than a half mile away.

"It's very bad out there, Dex," Jimmy said quietly. "This is the worst tornado I've ever seen. It's just miles and miles of destruction. Parts of Joplin are completely gone."

"Come with us to the hospital," Sara said. "We'll help you find your parents after we take care of Norm."

Dex was tempted. He didn't want to be alone.

But he couldn't wait. And Jimmy and Sara had no time to argue.

They hugged Dex as though they were all family.

Dex watched them drive off.

And now it was time for Dex to head into the ruins, to discover what was left.

CHAPTER 14

No matter where Dex looked, in every direction, as far as he could see, Joplin was in ruins. What was once his city — his peaceful, bustling city — had been shattered into millions of pieces.

He made his way into his neighborhood, where just yesterday he had been riding his bike. The streets were filled with downed wires and splintered telephone poles. The trees that had shaded him on hot summer days were now naked sticks, their leaves and branches carpeting the ground. Cars and trucks were everywhere but parked in driveways. They were crushed in the middle of the street, flipped upside down, wrapped around poles.

And then there were the houses.

Some had been swept away completely, so that only cement slabs remained. Others were chopped up, or cut in half, smashed by trees or peeled open. And what had been in people's kitchens and bedrooms and desk drawers and toy boxes was now scattered everywhere. Someone's family portrait, smudged with grime, smiled out from under a pile of plaster and jagged glass. A page from a children's book blew through the air like a dead leaf. A basketball rolled down the street, as though someone had just missed a free throw. Mixed in with the piles of wood and roof shingles were parts of couches, stuffed animals, a smashed oven, a headless Barbie doll, dishes, pots . . . parts of people's lives scattered like puzzle pieces. Everything was soaking wet and covered with brown filth.

Dex rounded the corner onto his street.

Or was it his street?

He couldn't know for sure, because there was nothing left.

He didn't see a soul.

He walked more quickly, gaping in horror at the wreckage of the Tuckers' house. He whispered a prayer of thanks as he remembered that the Tuckers had left yesterday. Their house was destroyed, but the Tuckers were safe in Arkansas.

He walked faster and faster, and soon he was running, until he reached the spot where his own house should have been.

Mom's car was upside down. Dad's station wagon was nowhere to be seen.

And the house.

The house where Dex had lived his whole life. The house where Dex had learned to walk and talk and tie his shoes and read and write, where he'd put his baby teeth under his pillow and waited for Santa to come down the chimney. The house where he rode around on Jeremy's shoulders, feeling like the luckiest boy on earth.

The house that had made him.

The tornado had smashed it to pieces, and now it was just a mountain of rubble.

And where were Mom and Dad?

Where was Zeke?

They would have taken shelter in the basement. And now they were trapped somewhere under the wreckage.

Dex climbed up the pile of ruins and dropped to his knees.

"Mom! Dad! Zeke!"

He grabbed hunks of wood and plaster that used to be his house and he started throwing them aside. There were bricks from the fireplace and huge shards of glass and broken plates and Dad's smashed laptop and an old baseball bat.

His whole body shook with sobs as he tore away at the wreckage, desperate to reach his family. He barely noticed that a huge nail was stabbing into his knee, and that both of his hands were dripping with blood.

Don't quit.

Don't quit.

Don't quit.

And then something touched his neck — something warm and slobbery.

Dex spun around.

He looked up, and there was Zeke standing behind him, balanced on a wooden beam.

He stared at his dog, his beautiful ugly dog who was soaking wet and covered with dirt and grime, whose tongue was hanging out of his mouth.

Where had he come from?

Zeke licked Dex again.

Dex threw his arms around his dog, burying his face in his filthy fur.

And then Dex heard voices calling from the street, ragged shouts that rose up over the sirens that wailed all across Joplin.

"Dex!"

"Dex!"

Dex jumped up and practically flew toward the street, with Zeke following right behind him.

Mom reached him first, and then Dad.

They all grabbed hold of one another, and Zeke nuzzled in, too.

They clung together and cried.

But they did not cry for what had been lost.

That would come later.

Right now, they were crying for what they had found.

CHAPTER 15

TWO WEEKS LATER
MONDAY, JUNE 6
7:00 A.M.

Dex sat up in bed, his heart pounding.

He'd heard a noise.

Was it the tornado siren?

He held his breath.

No.

It was just Dad's phone alarm.

Zeke was sprawled out next to Dex. He stared up with worried eyes, his ears pressed back.

82

"We're okay," Dex whispered, kissing Zeke on the head.

And they were.

Still, it took a minute for Dex's heart to stop pounding, for the nauseous swirl to clear from his stomach. Though he was sleeping better, the tornado howled through his dreams. And he always woke up in a sweaty panic, reliving the terror of the storm, the jumbled darkness of those first few days.

Joplin had been cut off from the world. Many of the roads were closed. Phones were dead and power blacked out. Every hour brought more terrible news. One hundred and fifty-eight were killed in the storm. They died in their homes, in stores, on the roads, in their cars. More than a thousand were wounded. So many families had lost everything they had.

Dex would never forget those terrifying minutes when he was sure Mom and Dad and Zeke were lost in the rubble. It turned out that Mom and Dad weren't in the house at all. They'd been driving home from the graduation when the sirens went off. Luckily they'd had enough time to pull the car over and sprint into the basement of a restaurant. Their car had been sucked away; they still hadn't been able to find it.

None of them wanted to think about what would have happened if anyone had been in the house when the tornado hit. What if Mom and Dad hadn't stayed after the graduation to help take pictures? What if Dex hadn't gone with Dr. Gage that day? What if they had been in the basement when the beams of their house cracked? A crushing mountain of wood and plaster and appliances and furniture had come crashing into the basement, filling every inch.

Nobody would have survived down there.

A big mystery was how Zeke made it through. None of them could figure out how he had suddenly just *appeared* when Dex was searching through the rubble.

It was Dr. Gage who had the best answer.

"I told you, your dog has superpowers," he'd said.

Dex smiled to himself, thinking of Dr. Gage safe at his house in Tulsa.

For an agonizing week after the storm, Dex had no idea whether Dr. Gage was alive or dead. Joplin's main hospital had been practically destroyed, and so Joplin's wounded were taken to hospitals for miles around. With no phone service, they had no way of tracking him down. Finally the call came from Sara: Dr. Gage was in a hospital in Oklahoma. He was still weak, but getting better every day.

Now that Dr. Gage was back at home, he and Dex spoke almost every day. They'd made a plan for Dex and Mom and Dad to visit him in Tulsa in a few weeks. Dex already had the present he would bring.

He'd retrieved it from the wreckage of Dr. Gage's SUV.

Dad had gone with him to the parking lot of Peter's Garage, to see if there was anything in the SUV they could salvage for Dr. Gage.

They found some maps, and some important papers in the glove compartment. And Dex discovered something else: the small hail freezer wedged under the front seat. Dex yanked it free. The battery-operated motor was still humming. And inside, that huge piece of hail was still frozen solid.

Dex lifted the glistening ball out of the freezer. At first he wanted to smash it into millions of pieces. That hailstone was part of the storm system that had destroyed his city!

Yes it was. And that's why Dex put it back in the little freezer, to save for Dr. Gage.

Who knew? Maybe there was some secret inside the icy ball, a clue that would help Dr. Gage unravel the mysteries of tornadoes.

Dex finally got out of bed. He got dressed,

squeezing around the boxes and bins stacked everywhere in their tiny apartment.

Each one was filled up with books and dishes and photos and other treasures they'd managed to salvage from the soggy wreckage of their house. For days they had sifted through the pile, with the help of volunteers from around the country. Thousands had flocked to Joplin to help pick up the pieces.

And of course people from Joplin were helping one another, too.

A friend of Dad's had found this apartment. Mike Sturm brought Dex a whole bag of clothes, some of them brand-new. Dylan and his family had donated a TV, some sheets and blankets, and this cot. Dylan had helped Dex get the bed set up, and of course they made it right, the SEAL way. They'd even smiled at each other, the kind of smiles they used to share back when they'd been best friends. It seemed the tornado had broken down that wall that had risen up between them.

And now Dex picked up the little box that was resting on the windowsill.

It had arrived in the mail yesterday, sent from a secret military base in some far-off country.

It was from Jeremy.

Dex's brother had managed to finally get in touch with them, three days after the storm. He spoke to Mom and Dad and then Dex finally had his turn.

"Jeremy!" he'd cried, fighting back tears.

At first there was only silence.

"Jer?"

Dex was about to hang up, figuring they'd been cut off.

But then came a choked-up whisper. "Dex . . ."

And Dex understood. His brother, his brave warrior brother, was crying.

That got Dex blubbering, too, but he didn't care. It was a while before either of them could get a word out.

But then they talked and talked and talked. And the call ended with the best news of all: that Jeremy's mission was ending. He would be home for a visit within the month.

Dex opened the box Jeremy had sent.

He stared at the sparkling gold trident pin.

Jeremy's SEAL pin.

"You earned this," Jeremy had written.

At first Dex couldn't believe Jeremy was giving it away. That trident was what made Jeremy a SEAL!

But no. It wasn't a piece of gold-painted metal that made Jeremy strong and brave.

It was what was inside him.

And wasn't the same true of Joplin?

What Dex loved about Joplin wasn't the buildings and the houses.

It was the faith of the people, their strength. A tornado couldn't break that.

Dex and Zeke stood at the window. Zeke's ears perked up at the buzzing of chainsaws and the booming of dump trucks and back hoes, the sounds of Joplin being put back together. Dex thought about his busy day ahead. The Tuckers were finally coming back to Joplin, and Dex was helping them move into their temporary house. Later on, he and Dylan and Mike were going to volunteer in the shelter organized by their church.

There was so much to do.

Dex's mission had just begun.

WHY I WROTE ABOUT
JOPLIN, MISSOURI

Whenever I go on a school visit, some nice reader asks me if I have a favorite I Survived book. I always give the same answer, and according to my eleven-year-old daughter, Valerie, it's a *bad* answer: I have no favorite book in the series.

I explain that, unlike many book series, each I Survived book takes me on a different journey. Each character is a new creation. By the time I am finished writing a book, my characters seem so real to me that I even dream about them. Not long ago, I had a dream that Oscar from my Chicago Fire book was sitting at my kitchen table eating tacos with our family. (He seemed to like them.)

So no, I don't have a favorite I Survived book because I love all of my characters equally, and each story has deep meaning to me.

But *The Joplin Tornado* is especially close to my heart because it was people from Joplin who suggested that I write it. And it was their true stories — dozens of them — that guided me. I visited Joplin and got to spend time with the wonderful librarians from Joplin's elementary schools. I met hundreds of kids and their teachers. Dex and his family are fictional characters, but many of their experiences were inspired by stories people shared with me.

Joplin is officially a city, but it feels more like a small town. It sits in the middle of America where three states touch: Missouri, Kansas, and Oklahoma. It's a pretty place, with an interesting history as a nineteenth-century lead mining town. The people are incredibly friendly — buying a tube of toothpaste at the local CVS felt like going to a family picnic. It was easy for me to see why so many people who are born here never leave.

The tornado that hit Joplin was the deadliest to hit America in fifty years. It was nearly one mile wide at its widest point, a rain-wrapped "multiple vortex" tornado, which means it had more than one funnel. Entire neighborhoods were completely swept away; 158 people were killed, more than 1,100 wounded. Thousands of people lost their homes. Five schools and a major hospital were destroyed, along with hundreds of businesses.

Four years later, the city has been almost completely rebuilt. Librarian Ashley Tucker, my kind and generous guide during my visit to Joplin, drove me through some of the heavily damaged areas. The most obvious scars from the tornado are some still-empty lots and skeleton trees that stand amid the newly built houses and beautiful schools. Otherwise it was hard to imagine that just three and a half years before my visit, one-third of the city lay in ruins.

Within people's minds, though, the memories of that day are still raw. So many lost relatives and neighbors. People described the tornado's howling roar, the power of its fierce winds, the terror of feeling their homes collapsing around them as they huddled in a basement or bathtub or closet.

Being in Joplin, I kept thinking about another question I often get from my young readers: Why do I choose to write about disasters and other such dark and frightening events? One boy just wrote to me today, "Mrs. Tarshis, no offense, but why do you write about such DEPRESSING subjects?"

Here's my answer, one that my daughter approves of: The I Survived series isn't really about disasters. It's about people. Yes, I write long chapters filled with destruction. But in the end, my books are about *resilience* — the ability most of us have to recover after experiencing something difficult or painful.

Within minutes of the tornado strike, the people of Joplin were helping one another. Neighbors searched for neighbors. People with pickup trucks took to the streets looking for people who needed to get to the hospital. Thousands of volunteers from around the country flocked to Joplin to help with the cleanup and recovery. Many of the people I spoke to, including kids, told me that their experiences on May 22, 2011, strengthened their faith, their bonds with their family, and their appreciation for life's gifts.

To me, that's the story of Joplin.

I feel honored to share it with all of you.

A TIME LINE OF THE
JOPLIN TORNADO

Saturday, May 14

A mass of cold, dry air that was born in the Gulf of Alaska travels down the West Coast to California. It moves east, crossing the Rocky Mountains. In eastern Colorado, it collides with a stream of warm, moist air that blew up from the Gulf of Mexico. A violent storm system is born.

Sunday, May 15

The system unleashes a powerful thunderstorm across Colorado. Small tornadoes touch down east of Denver.

Saturday, May 21

The system gains strength as it marches east into Kansas. At 9:15 P.M., a tornado touches down in the tiny town of Reading, population 231. It severely damages the downtown. A fifty-three-year-old man is killed.

Sunday, May 22

The day dawns bright and clear in Joplin, Missouri. There are forecasts for thunderstorms for later in the afternoon.

1:30 P.M.: The National Weather Service issues a tornado watch for Joplin and surrounding areas. A tornado *watch* means that the conditions are right for tornadoes, but that there is no specific threat.

2:00 P.M.: The storm system moves into eastern Kansas. Fifty miles northwest of Joplin, it forms a violent supercell, which unleashes rain and hail over the town of Parsons.

4:30 P.M.: There is so much energy in the air that two more supercells develop to the south of the main storm. In Columbus, Kansas, twenty-five miles northwest of Joplin, rain and baseball-size hail fall from the sky. The three supercells begin to move east, toward Joplin.

5:00 P.M.: The National Weather Service issues a tornado warning for areas in Missouri, Kansas, and Oklahoma. A tornado *warning* is more severe than a tornado watch. It means that a threat is imminent — that a tornado is almost certainly coming — and that people should take shelter. But this warning covers only the northeastern portion of Joplin, and weather forecasts suggest that the worst of the storm will hit north of the city.

5:11 P.M.: Joplin's twenty-eight tornado sirens wail. They sound for three minutes and then go silent. No tornadoes touch down.

5:17 P.M.: A new tornado warning is issued that includes all of Joplin.

5:20 P.M.: Four young storm chasers, driving on a road four miles west of Joplin, witness the moment when wisps of clouds transform into a black churning tornado. Within minutes, the tornado is wrapped in a curtain of rain. It is completely invisible as it heads into Joplin.

5:30 P.M.: Another team of storm chasers, Jeff and Kathryn Piotrowski, is following a storm into Joplin. The two are among the first to realize that the gray cloud to the west is a massive rain-wrapped tornado. Jeff stops to alert a Joplin policeman, who is sitting in a parked car. "Get the sirens going," Piotrowski warns.

5:31 P.M.: Joplin's sirens sound a second time.

5:32 P.M.: The tornado, now three-fourths of a mile wide, begins its attack on Joplin.

5:43 P.M.: Weather forecasters stare in shock at their radar screens; the area above southern Joplin is filled with pink splotches, indicating debris from the city that a tornado has thrown thousands of feet into the sky.

The tornado grinds on for thirteen more miles, laying waste to a third of Joplin.

6:12 P.M.: The tornado disappears into the sky.

QUESTIONS AND ANSWERS ABOUT TORNADOES

I learned so much about tornado science and storm chasing while researching this book. Here are the answers to just a few questions that might be on your mind.

Where do tornadoes strike?

Tornadoes have touched down in every part of the world except Antarctica (as far as scientists know). But the vast majority of tornadoes happen in the United States. Since scientists started keeping track, the United States has been struck by ten times as many tornadoes as Canada, which ranks second. Half of all US tornadoes hit in the central plains; the area from northern Texas to North Dakota has often been called Tornado Alley. The South is another tornado-prone area in the United States. Mississippi has actually been hit by twice as many tornadoes as Kansas. But every state except Alaska has been struck by tornadoes.

How often do tornadoes strike in the United States?

An average of 1,000 tornadoes touch down in the United States every year. But in some years, there are far more. The year 2011 was unusually active; 1,691 tornadoes touched down, including 758 in April alone. On April 27, 2011, 200 tornadoes struck in that one day, the largest daily total ever recorded.

What causes tornadoes to form?

Scientists have been studying tornadoes for 150 years, but these storms remain one of the great mysteries of science. We know that tornadoes are created within violent supercell thunderstorms. But not all supercells give birth to tornadoes, and scientists have no way of predicting which storms will unleash deadly twisters and which ones will fade away.

What do storm chasers really do?

Storm chasing is very dangerous, and nobody should attempt to chase a storm unless they are very experienced. Many storm chasers are scientists determined to learn more about how tornadoes work. Storm chasers are actually an important part of America's tornado warning system. Weather forecasters don't know for sure that a tornado exists until it actually touches down. Very often, the first to see a tornado are storm chasers, who notify police and weather forecasters so that people can be warned.

The character of Dr. Gage is based on three chasers I discovered in my research. Tim Samaras spent years trying to record sounds from inside tornadoes. And Jeff and Kathryn Piotrowski spotted the tornado as it was closing in on Joplin. It was Jeff who alerted the police, who called for the tornado sirens to be sounded for the second time that day. Very likely their work saved lives.

Tragically, Tim Samaras, who was famous for his caution, was killed in May 2013, when his car was overtaken by a rain-wrapped tornado in El Reno, Oklahoma.

STAYING SAFE IN A TORNADO

Get informed.

Go to the website Ready.gov.

Read the tornado safety information carefully (have your parents read it, too!).

You will learn everything you need to know there, but here are some especially important tips:

- Be aware of the weather, especially if you live in a tornado-prone area and during the spring and summer, when most tornadoes strike.
- If the weather looks stormy, look and listen for weather alerts on TV, a reliable weather website, or a local radio station.
- Take tornado watches and warnings seriously. If you are urged to take shelter, do it immediately.
- Go inside if there is danger of a tornado (there is really no safe place outdoors in a tornado).
- Stay away from windows and do not open them.
- The safest place in a building is a basement. If there is no basement, take shelter in an interior

room on the building's lowest level, away from corners, windows, doors, and outside walls. Try to get under a very heavy table or desk. Cover your head with your hands to protect yourself from flying debris.

- Cars and trucks are not ever safe in a tornado. But if you are caught (as Dex was), buckle your seat belt and cover your head with your hands.
- If you are taking shelter at home, put on a bike or ski helmet. This might sound silly, but storm chasers wear them when there is danger of flying debris.

FOR FURTHER READING
AND LEARNING

Here are some resources I found if you'd like to explore further.

To see the path of the Joplin tornado:

http://www.tripline.net/trip/Path_of_the
_Joplin_Tornado-0424207775021003AD43C13
C53060EBC

My inspiration for making Jeremy a Navy SEAL was a speech written by Admiral William H. McRaven. He gave the speech at the graduation ceremony at the University of Texas, Austin, on May 17, 2014. You can (and should) read it for yourself right here:

http://www.utexas.edu/news/2014/05/16/admiral
-mcraven-commencement-speech

Some tornado books for you:

Disaster Strikes: Tornado Alley, by Marlane Kennedy, New York, NY: Scholastic Inc., 2014

DK Eyewitness: Hurricane & Tornado, by Jack Challoner, New York, NY: DK Publishing, 2004

Inside Tornadoes, by Mary Kay Carson, New York, NY: Sterling Publishing, 2010

Tornado!: The Story Behind These Twisting, Turning, Spinning, and Spiraling Storms, by Judith Bloom Fradin and Dennis Brindell Fradin, Washington, D.C.: National Geographic, 2011

Selected Bibliography for *I Survived the Joplin Tornado, 2011*

These are the sources I relied on most heavily in my research.

Black Hawk Down: A Story of Modern War, by Mark Bowden, New York, NY: Atlantic Monthly Press, 1999. Paperback reprint, New York: Grove Press, 2010

"The Gathering Storm," by Cindy Hoedel and

Lisa Gutierrez, *Kansas City Star*, December 9, 2011

"Heavenly Father! . . ." by Luke Dittrich, *Esquire*, September 22, 2011

Hunting Nature's Fury: A Storm Chaser's Obsession with Tornadoes, Hurricanes, and Other Natural Disasters, by Roger Hill with Peter Bronski, Berkeley, CA: Wilderness Press, 2009

"The Last Chase," by Robert Draper, *National Geographic*, November 2013

No Hero: The Evolution of a Navy SEAL, by Mark Owen with Kevin Maurer, New York, NY: Dutton, 2014

"*Storm Chasing the Joplin EF-5 Tornado*," created by Jeff and Kathryn Piotrowski. *Journey Through Tornado Alley* series. (Storm Productions Inc., 2011), DVD. TwisterChasers.com

Storm Kings: The Untold History of America's First Tornado Chasers, by Lee Sandlin, New York: Pantheon Books, 2013

Stormstalker blog (stormstalker.wordpress.com)

Tornado Alley: Monster Storms of the Great Plains,

by Howard B. Bluestein, New York: Oxford University Press, 1999

Tornado Hunter: Getting Inside the Most Violent Storms on Earth, by Stefan Bechtel with Tim Samaras, Washington, D.C.: National Geographic, 2009

Tornado Warning: The Extraordinary Women of Joplin, by Tamara Hart Heiner, Pikeville, NC: Dancing Lemur Press, 2014

Warnings: The True Story of How Science Tamed the Weather, by Mike Smith, Austin, TX: Greenleaf Book Group Press, 2010

When the Sirens Were Silent: How the Warning System Failed a Community, by Mike Smith, Wichita, KS: Mennonite Press/Mike Smith Enterprises, LLC, 2012

Witness: Joplin Tornado, documentary video by National Geographic Channel, https://www.youtube.com/watch?v=V_oyBGrxfpg